I DEDICATE THIS BOOK to my daughter, Anna Maybelle Cash.
Annabelle, you have taught me to love in a way I have never known before.
You are the direct and complete inspiration for this book.
May your real life be bigger than your dreams.

ACKNOWLEDGMENTS: Gracious thanks to Kate Etue—thanks for hanging strong.
Thank you, Lou Robin, Laura Cash, and Jack and Joseph Cash.
Thanks to all the crew at Simon & Schuster—Jon Anderson, Jeanie Lee,
Sonali Fry, and Valerie Garfield—and to Rick Richter and Dee Ann Grand.
And once again to Marc—you have the ability to see the magic beyond the words.

–J. C. C.

To my beautiful wife, Janice, and her father, Guy,
who loved his little girl with all his heart.

–M. B.

🌅 LITTLE SIMON INSPIRATIONS

An imprint of Simon & Schuster Children's Publishing Division • 1230 Avenue of the Americas, New York, New York 10020
Text copyright © 2010 by John Carter Cash • Illustrations copyright © 2010 by Marc Burckhardt • Book design by Leyah Jensen
LITTLE SIMON INSPIRATIONS and associated colophon are trademarks of Simon & Schuster, Inc.
For information about special discounts for bulk purchases, please contact Simon & Schuster Special Sales at 1-866-506-1949
or business@simonandschuster.com. • The Simon & Schuster Speakers Bureau can bring authors to your live event.
For more information or to book an event contact the Simon & Schuster Speakers Bureau at 1-866-248-3049 or visit our
website at www.simonspeakers.com. • Manufactured in Mexico • 0410 RR6 • First Edition • 10 9 8 7 6 5 4 3 2 1
Library of Congress Cataloging-in-Publication Data: Cash, John Carter. • Daddy loves his little girl / by John Carter Cash ;
illustrated by Marc Burckhardt. — 1st ed. • p. cm. • Summary: From the deepest ocean to skies of blue, a father's love for his
child is without bounds. • ISBN 978-1-4169-7482-6 • [1. Stories in rhyme. 2. Father and child—Fiction. 3. Love—Fiction.]
I. Burckhardt, Marc, 1962- ill. II. Title. • PZ8.3.C2713Dad 2010 • [E]—dc22 • 2008051297

JOHN CARTER CASH

Daddy Loves His Little Girl

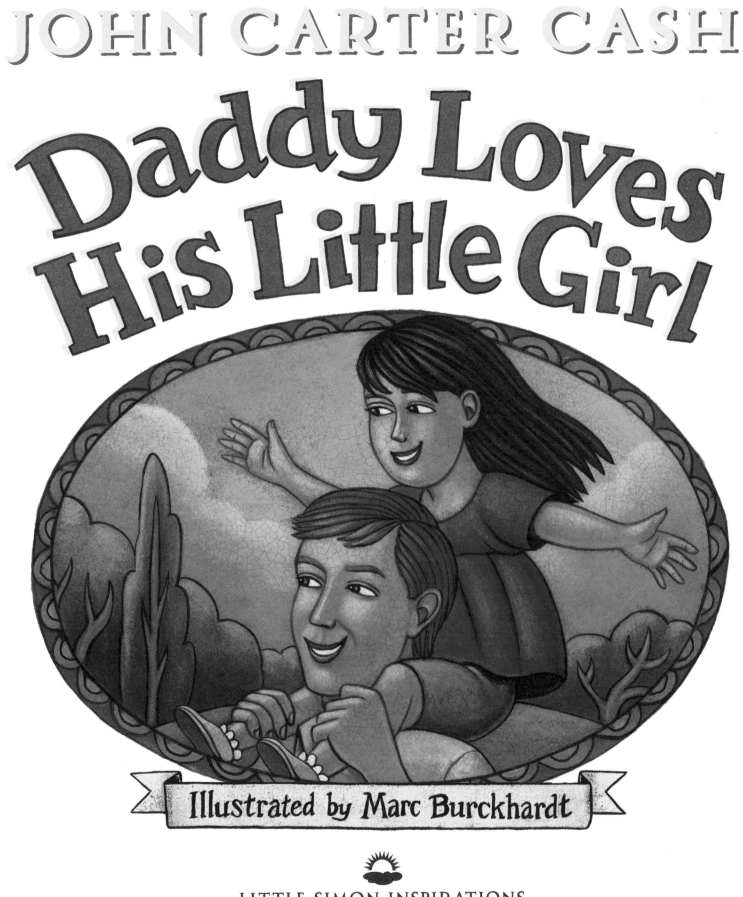

Illustrated by Marc Burckhardt

LITTLE SIMON INSPIRATIONS
New York   London   Toronto   Sydney

Daddy loves his little girl,
with arms spread open wide.
He cherishes the love you give
and holds it deep inside.

Daddy loves his little girl,
deep as the ocean blue.
Wide as the mighty river,
forever he'll love you.

He'll tell stories to his princess
of a far-off magic land

where he'll build a castle by the sea
of golden shells and sand.

When you're up on Daddy's shoulders,
he'll raise your flag up high.

Around the castle he'll dig a moat
where gators can swim by.

And . . . if pirates storm this fortress strong,
an eagle will fly by

to rescue you and fly you off
into the bright blue sky.

He'll lead you to enchanted hills
just south of Kathmandu.

The king and queen, so wise and brave,
will bring great gifts to you.

Upon your head they'll place a crown
and offer you the throne.

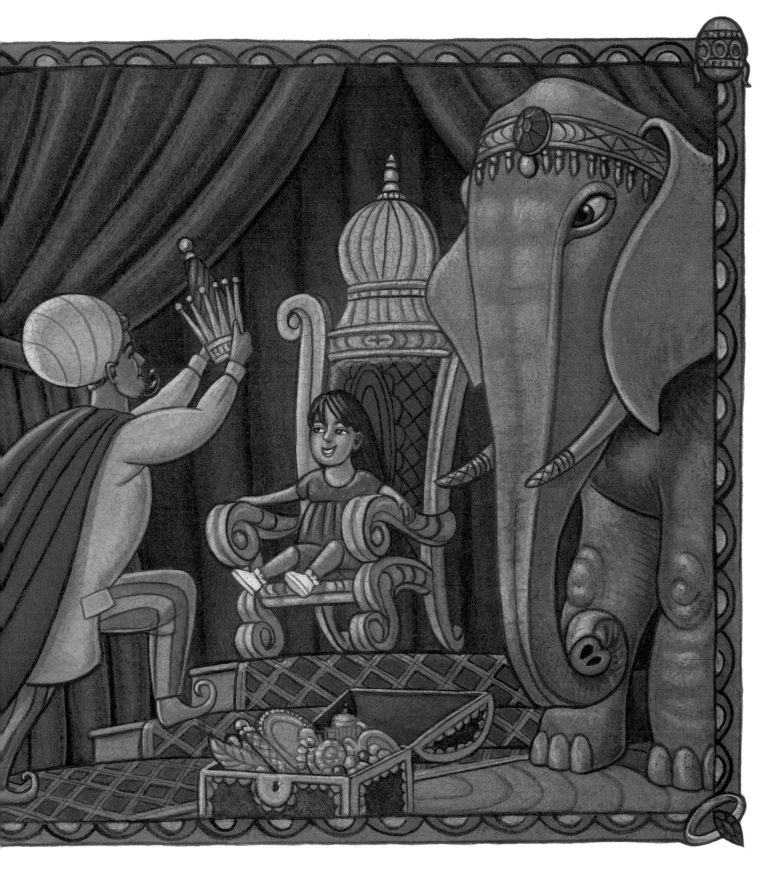

They'll give you shiny golden gems
and treasures few have known.

You'll feast on cakes stacked ten feet high,
and dance to Bluebird's whistles.

You'll run faster than the tiger
through the flowers and the thistles.

Then they'll have a grand parade—
the greatest in the land!

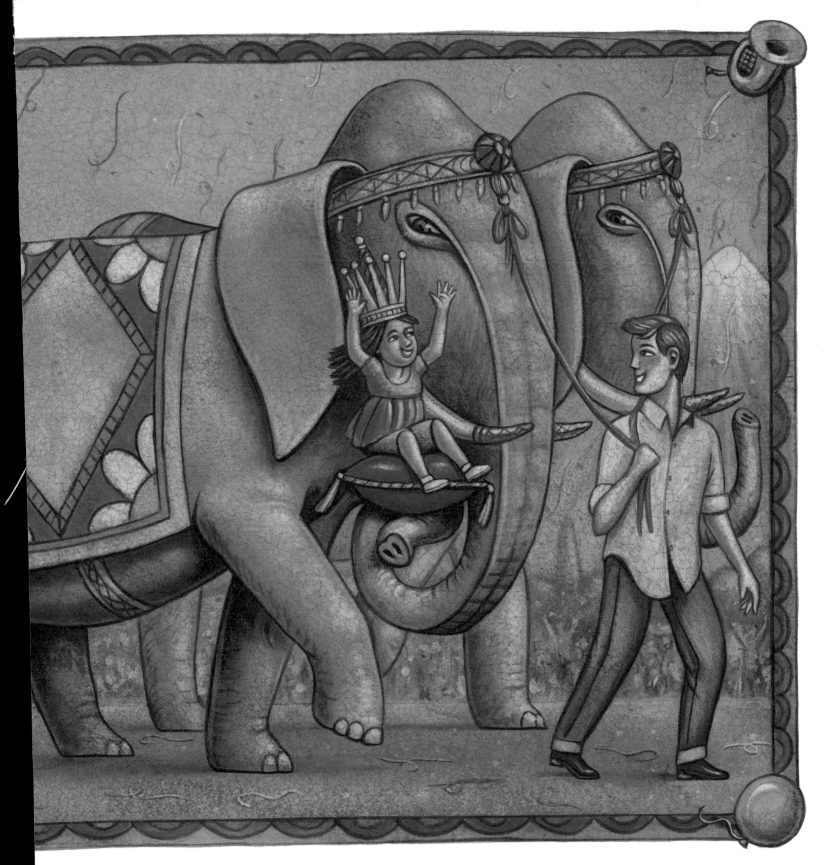

As flags and ribbons wave on high,
you'll lead a thousand-drummer band.

But when the sun begins to set,
the eagle will fly through.

Our old friend will guide us home
where Momma waits for you.

Remember this when bedtime nears
and Daddy says good night:
He loves you to the deepest depth
and to the greatest height.

Daddy loves his little girl
beyond the bounds of love.
You're the greatest treasure in the world,
and a blessing from above.